U0141063

世界现代广告设计经典

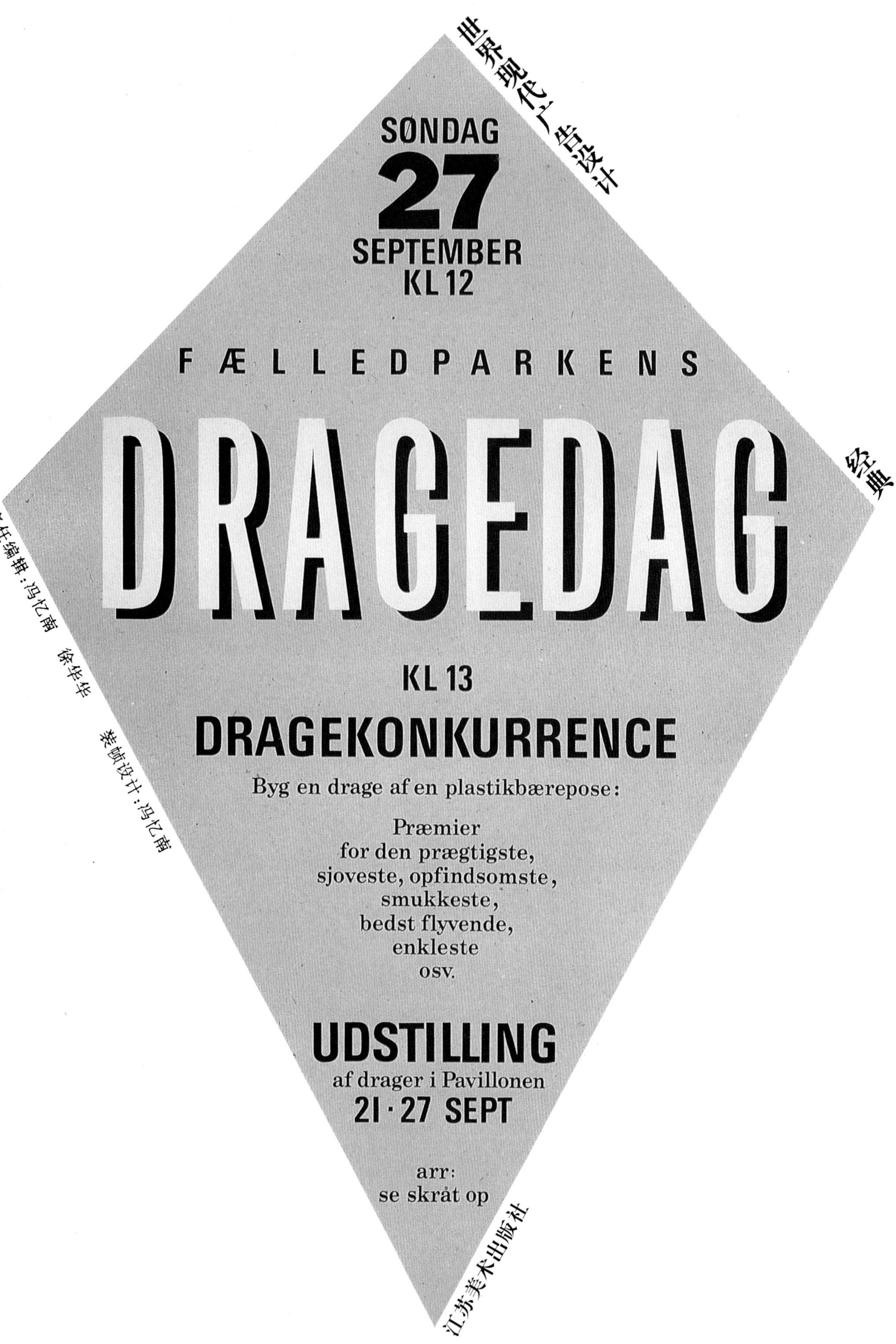

责任编辑：冯亿南　徐华华
装帧设计：冯亿南
江苏美术出版社

绪　言

　　广告设计艺术和纯艺术有相近点，但不同于纯艺术。首先，它要具备公共传播与交流的目的，使其宣传的主题能引起大众的广泛注意；其次，这一主题完成又是对应广告委托商的需求所作。广告对企业的宣传、商品的促销、演剧的火爆、竞选竞赛的壮烈等等商业活动产生积极的效应，因此，广告设计只能充分体现广告委托商所需主题的本质含意，为特定的集团做目的明确的宣传，不可能如纯艺术那样地具有能自主地创造崭新的形象及改变宣传方向的权力。

　　广告画，它具有与大众相沟通的功能，所反映的内容和表现的思想都是一个时代和一个社会的某种状况的记录，广告能敏感地捕捉住社会变革和进步的脉搏。从早期俄国革命所产生的构成主义，法国文化成熟期的装饰艺术趣味，德国的合理主义所萌生的包豪斯流派及法西斯专制抬头期的新古典主义风格，至战后现代艺术的中心移向美国带来的设计辉煌等等，在广告设计的发展中无不打上时代的烙印。

　　在今天，广告设计的创作，往往是由一个艺术性群体来操作完成。设计艺术家、插图画家或摄影家、雕塑家、文案撰稿者等等，根据制作的各种需要而进行最合理的搭配，在这里，一切艺术手段都服从于广告创意的特有需要，也就是在这里，纯艺术才变成为广告的艺术，并发出它特有的光辉。

　　在这里，我们从近一个世纪世界著名设计家的大批优秀作品中精选出部分做集中的介绍，希望能给读者带来学习和借鉴的方便，对专业广告设计界起到一个沟通信息的作用。我们期望，不远的将来，中国的设计家将进入世界最优秀的设计家行列。

　　　　　　　　　　　　　　　吕凤显

安迪·沃霍尔作品展广告

工业设计陈列广告

Radiererer
RadiIererInnen

im Kunst
Kunst
Kabinett
nett

Stockerenweg 3

beim Breitenrainplatz

3014 Bern

30. Mai 1988 bis 10. Juni 1988

Öffnungszeiten:

Montag bis Freitag

10.00 bis 12.00 Uhr

14.00 bis 17.00 Uhr

18 RadiererInnen

Roland Aellig

Sabine Abbassi

Martin Bähler

Claude Barbey

Hilmar Gottwald

Ursula Hürlimann

Herbert Iten

Kläri Lüthi

Bettina Kramer

Susanne Marti

Susanne Messerli

Heinz Pfister

Lotti Pulver

Hans Rüttimann

Daniel Scheidegger

Annegabi Schmidt

Silvia Schmidt

Kari Wismer

Gestaltung Lis Gürtig

Druckerei Aberegg Scheer K.

Siegigraphie Kunter AG

Kunsthaus
Zürich
12. März bis
23. Mai 1988

Schweizerische
Stiftung für
die Photographie

Photographien
Filme
Frühe Objekte

M A N

R A Y

Man Ray: Femme aux longs cheveux, 1929 Design: Werner Jeker Serigraphie: Albin Uldry

莫洛斯基 艺术展

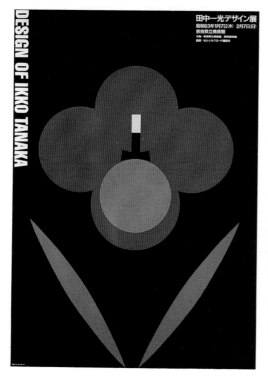

田中一光设计展

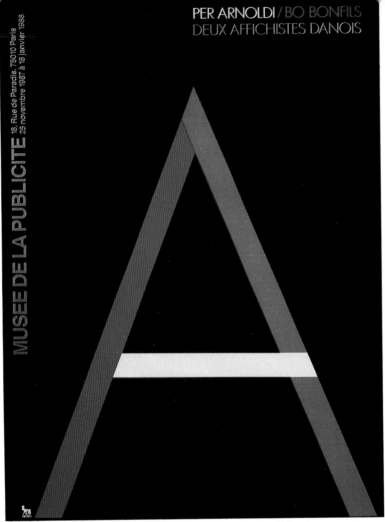

巴黎公众画展

苏黎世美术馆米罗画展广告

戏剧招贴

1927 年伦敦地铁

美国杰克逊公园广告

意大利电影节

音乐会招贴

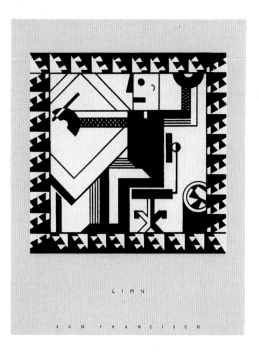

宣传广告

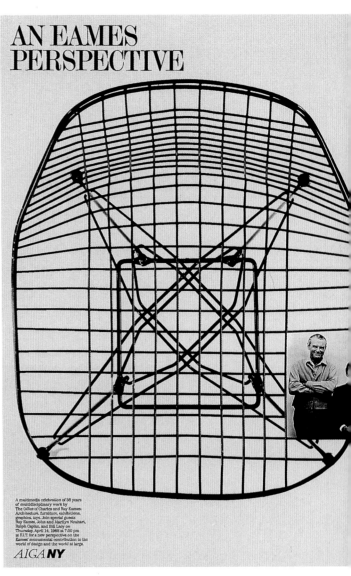

设计广告　宣传广告

犹太人

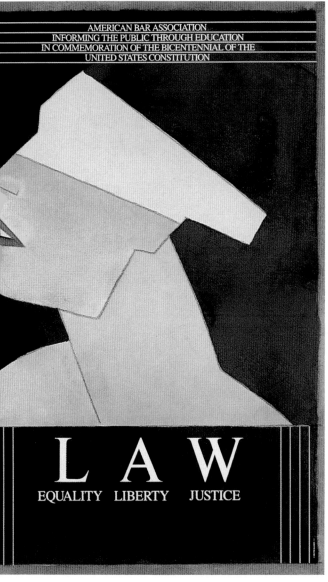

1987 年欧洲律师年会广告

平等・自由・公正

PIERRE GAGNAIRE RESTAURANT

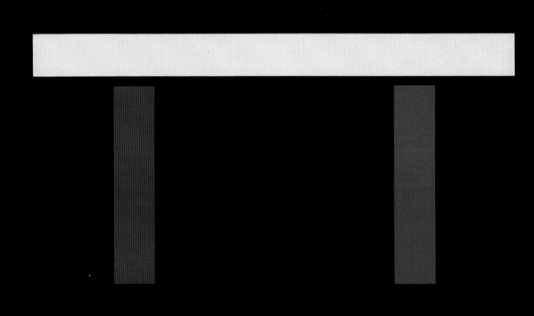

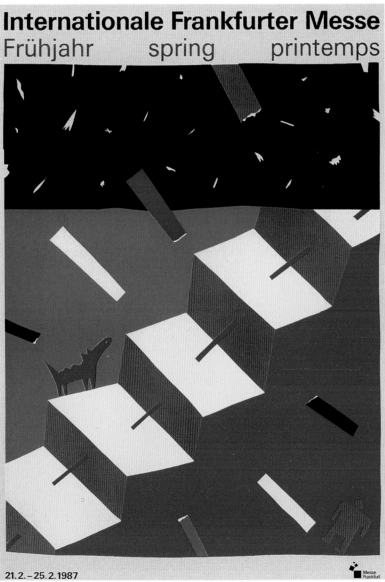

南方旅游快车

法兰克福国际博览会广告

Bühnen der Stadt Gera

SPARTACUS

Ballett von Aram Chatschaturjan · Choreographie Inge Berg-Peters · Kostüme Christa Hahn · Bühnenbild Theo Hug · Dramaturgie Wolfgang Ra

芭
蕾
舞

视觉艺术学校广告

世界重量级拳击冠军战

柔道比赛广告

现代与未来

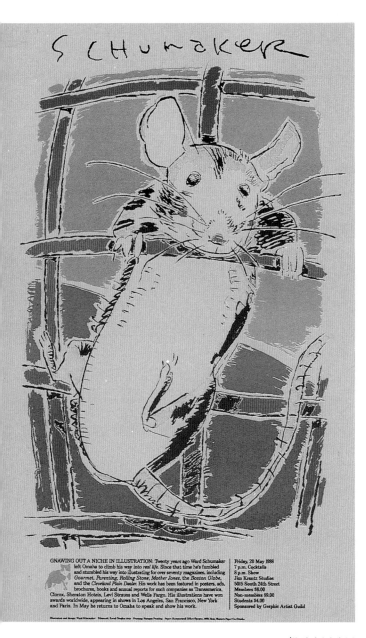 

舒马克图片展　　夏令营广告

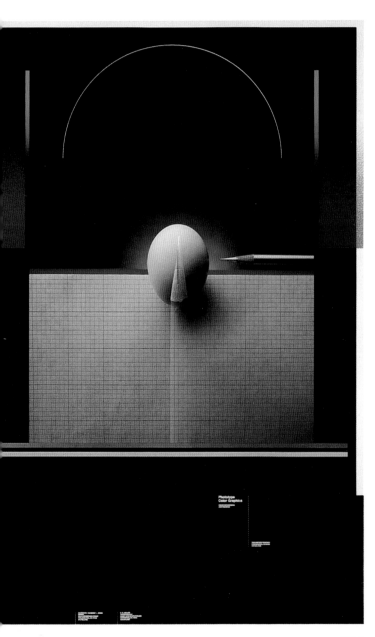
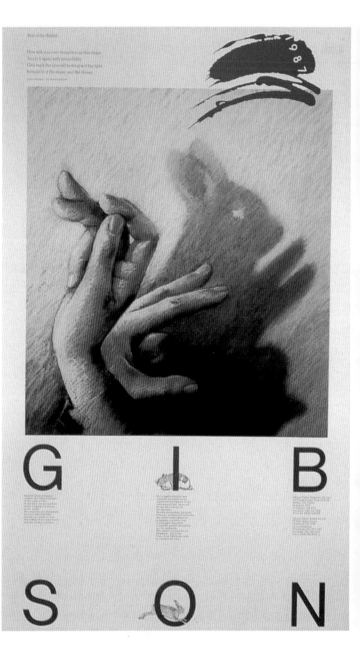

插图　宣传广告

视觉艺术学校广告

纽约拉瓜迪亚社区学院招生广告

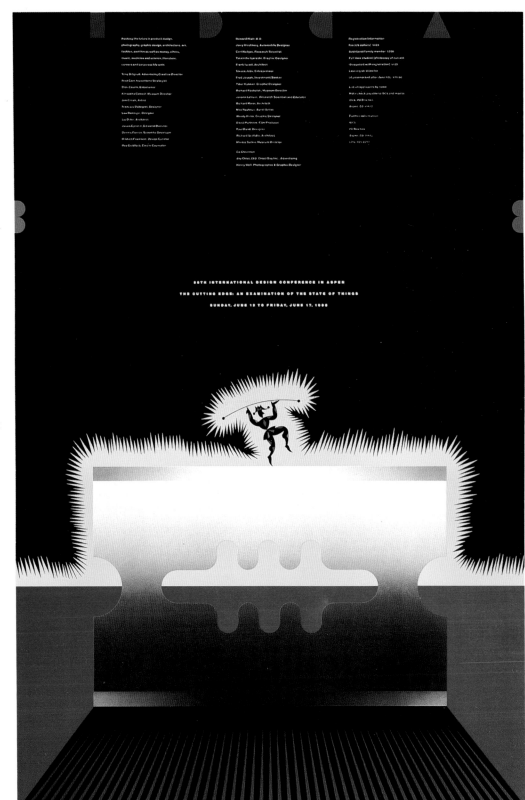

创新展

International Year of Graphic Design. 25th Anniversary of **ICOGRADA**, International Council of Graphic Design Associations.

1988 年国际平面设计展广告

设计

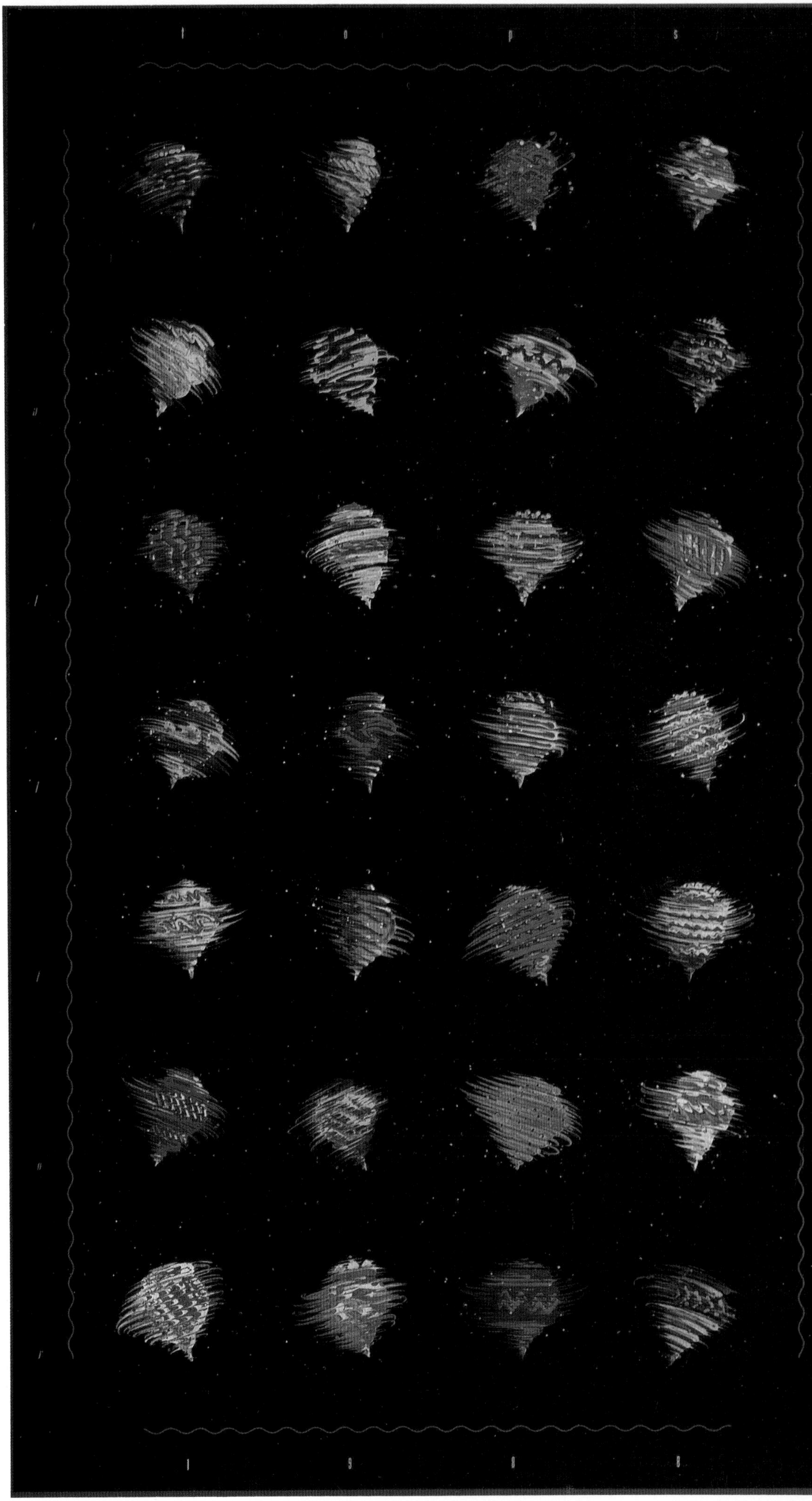

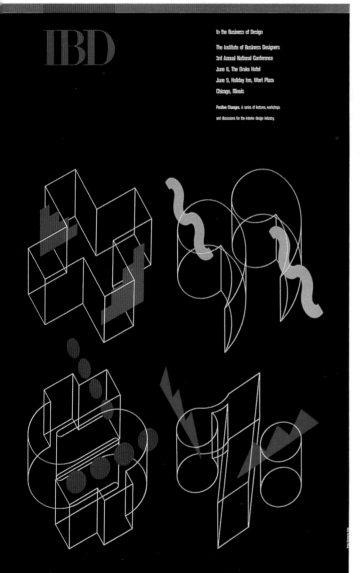

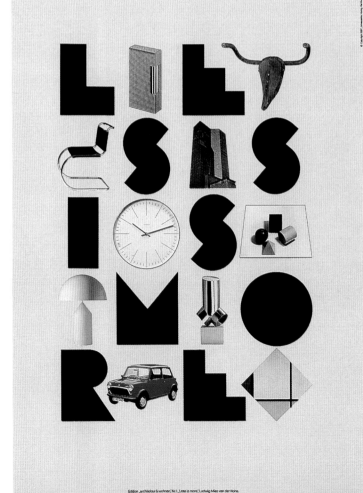

ГРАФИК ДИЗАЙН

Выставка графических работ
преподавателей и студентов вуза
графики и книгоискусства города Лейпцига
‹основан в 1764 ом году как академия
рисунка, живописи и архитектуры›

Факультет книгоискусства/
прикладной графики
ГДР 7010 Лейпциг, ул. Димитрова, 11
телефон 3 91 32 11

Профили подготовки:
полное оформление книг всех видов,
книжный переплёт, книжная иллюстрация,
каталог, журнал, плакат,
обложка грампластинки, календарь,

фирменный знак, деловые письма,
почтовая марка, печатный шрифт,
каллиграфия, архитектурная роспись,
упаковка, промышленная реклама,
проспект, выставочная графика

Министерства культуры ГДР/СССР
Дворец молодёжи, Москва
11.10. – 12.11.1989

宣传广告

圣弗兰西斯科现代艺术博物馆新址通告

Improve Your Image

FONTS

ion

page

printing

Leading the e... are not only breaki... aesthetic print quality for... crisp. But today's business... the quality of each printed page... symbolize the high standards, pro... leadership, and financial strength be... the quality of each printed page is a functio... Leading the electronic revolution in printing, too... are not only breaking the barriers of speed and re... aesthetic print quality for computer-generated outp...

...g, today's ion page p...ers... ...d and reliability, they are ... ...nd output. Yes... ...m...gibility. B... ...pora...mage. It s... ...ality...smans... ...n...sim... ...l...lea...

爱你的形象

和平

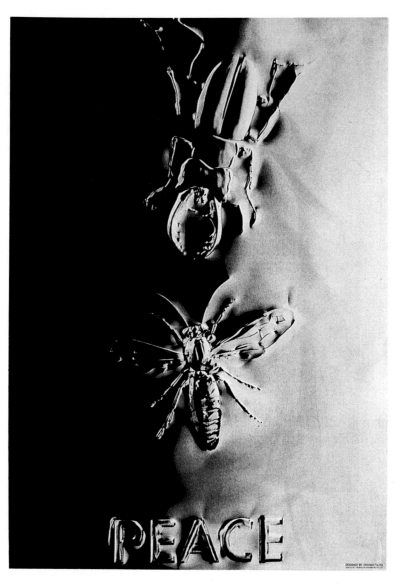

FOTOS FÜR MILLIONEN

大众形象摄影图片展

Eine Ausstellung der
Josef-Haubrich-Kunsthalle in Zusammenarbeit
mit dem Kölnischen Kunstverein.
Vom 3. Oktober bis 6. November 1988.

7 Bilderschauen
im Rahmen des Kodak Kulturprogramms:

ODYSSEE - Die schönsten Fotos aus National Geographic
40 JAHRE ZEITGESCHEHEN - 40 Jahre STERN
DIE ZEIT IM BILD - Fotojournalismus in Amerika
DIE KUNST, MIT BILDERN ZU ÜBERZEUGEN - Eine Geschichte der Werbefotografie
YOU PRESS THE BUTTON - WE DO THE REST. Aus den Kindertagen der Schnappschußfotografie
AUGENZEUGEN - World Press Photo 1988
DIE WAHRHEIT BEKENNT FARBE - Contact Press Images

Täglich von 10 bis 17 Uhr, Di. und Fr. bis 20 Uhr.
Verlängerte Öffnungszeiten
während der photokina (4. + 6. bis 11. 10.):
täglich 10 bis 20 Uhr.

Stadt Köln

展览广告

美国加州工艺博物馆动物标本展广告

展览广告

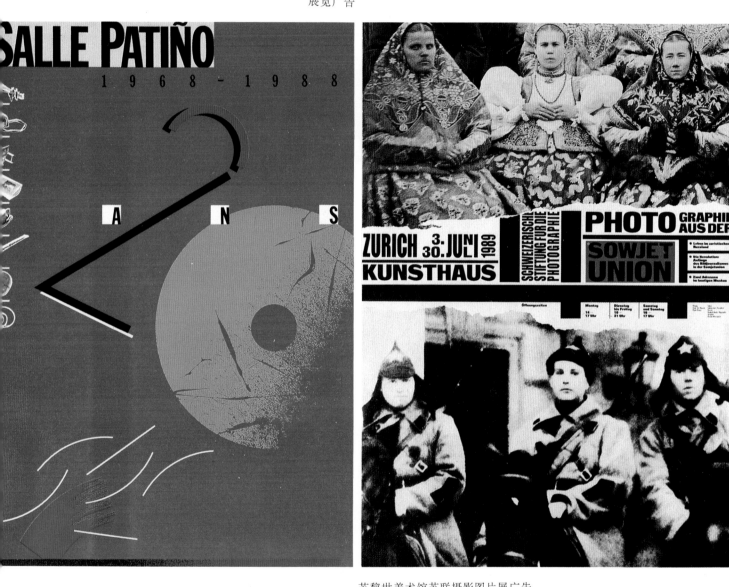

苏黎世美术馆苏联摄影图片展广告

RAZSTAVA '88
DRUŠTVA
OBLIKOVALCEV
SLOVENIJE

LIKOVNO RAZSTAVIŠČE
RIHARD JAKOPIČ
LJUBLJANA
KARDELJEVA 12

22. DECEMBER 1988
DO 6. JANUAR 1989

宣传广告

乡村西部音乐

"Oh, #@*$! Who am I going to get for speaker at our next meeting? ✳;#★, it's only four weeks away and I said I'd come up with someone who could talk about creativity and really motivate our whole group. What ever possessed me to take this assignment? Now I'm really up $;✳\"@'# creek!" Sound familiar? Don't worry. Just pick up the phone and dial 203-384-9443. Ask for Andy Goodman. He's President/General Manager of The American Comedy Network, a radio syndication company which currently supplies original comedy features to over 275 stations across the United States and Canada. Since 1983, Andy has served as head writer for ACN, honing the unique skills of communicating and being funny with sound. For the last 2 years, Andy has been crisscrossing the country talking to groups like yours about two important subjects: "The Power of Sound" and "Writing Funny." "The Power of Sound" is a 45-minute presentation that dramatically demonstrates radio's unique ability to reach people's hearts and minds like no other medium can. Broadcasters and advertisers alike have found the talk inspirational in making them rethink the ways they use the medium of radio. "Writing Funny" (also known as "A Workshop for Sit-down Comics") is a 1-hour seminar that teaches people how to unlock their own creativity and "write funny" on deadline – for radio, TV, or print. Most importantly, it gives you definitive, useable techniques you can begin applying to your work immediately. So, if you're planning a "Radio Day," a monthly Ad Club luncheon, evening program, a meeting of a single radio station or a large group of stations, don't panic. Give Andy a call and ask for more information about "The Power of Sound" or "Writing Funny." He may be just the speaker you've been looking for. No shit.

五十年中国新闻摄影集

铜管音乐会广告

反战广告

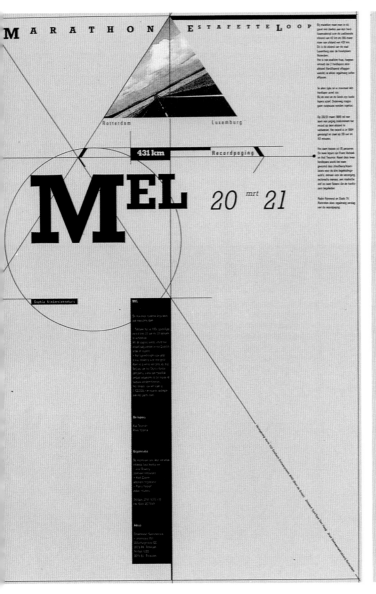

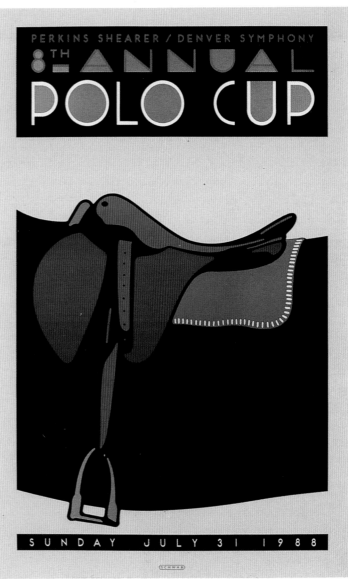

卢卡 土耳其前卫艺术展广告

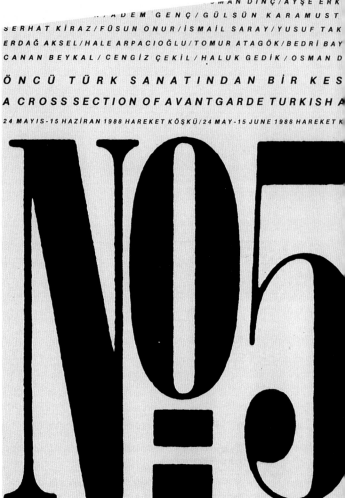

宣传广告

EAST

9/20 HARRISON/BLANCHARD QUINTET FULL CIRCLE

9/21 KIRK WHALUM KIMIKO ITOH

9/22 THE GADD GANG EDDIE GOMEZ

MEETS

WEST

9/23 STEVE SMITH & VITAL INFORMATION BRIAN SLAWSON

9/24 BRANFORD MARSALIS HARRY CONNICK, JR. OSAMU

9/25 NANCY WILSON MASAHIKO SATOH

LIVE AT THE BOTTOMLINE

A PRESENTATION OF AMC INTERNATIONAL • IN COOPERATION WITH: EPIC/SONY, INC. • CBS RECORDS, INC. • SONY CORPORATION TELEPHONE: (212) 228-6300

东方与西方的交汇——音乐系列演奏广告

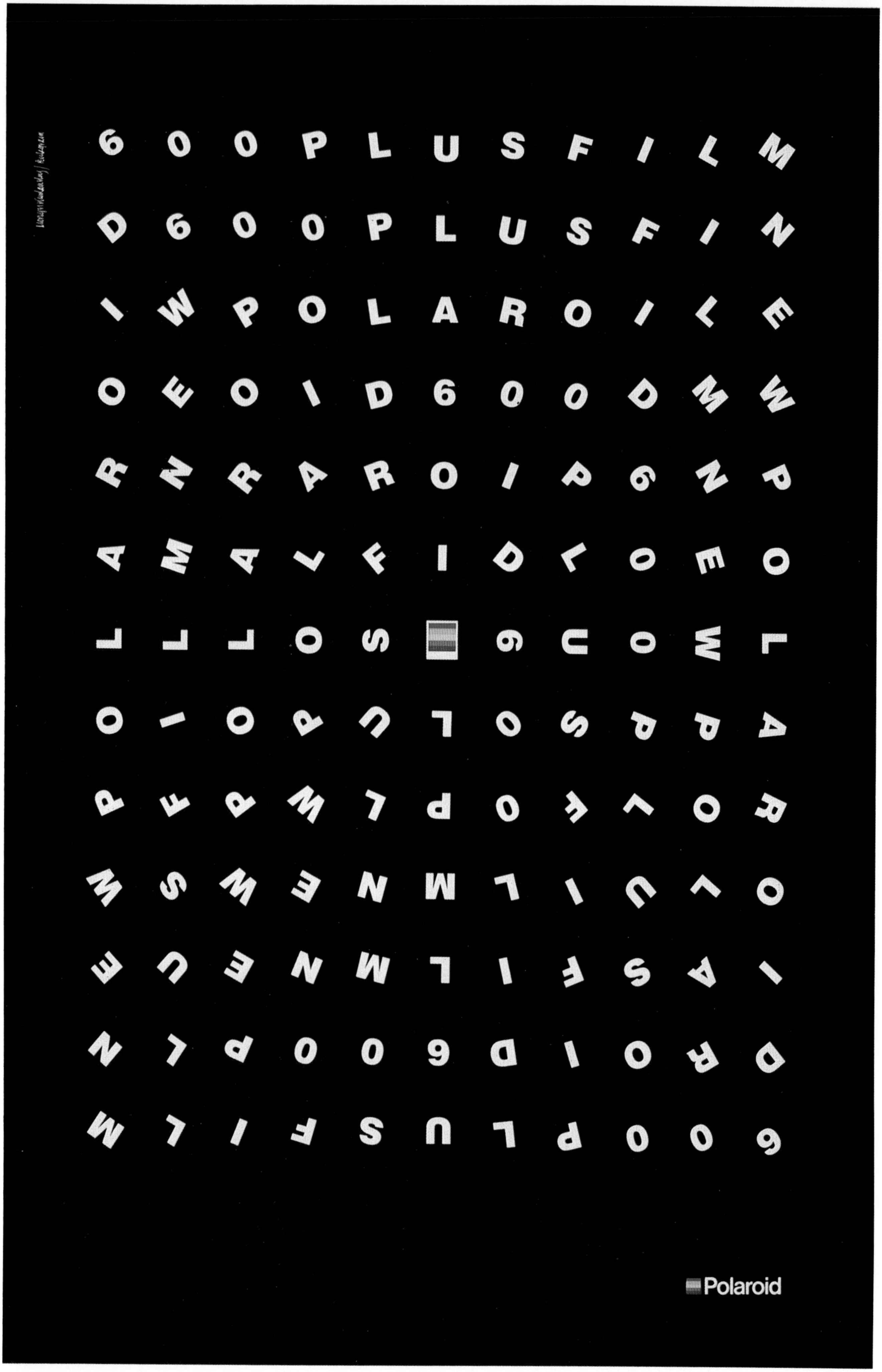

胶卷公司广告

The 1988 World's Most Memorable Poster
Jan 24 - Feb 8 Western Merchandise Mart

1988 年世界招贴作品展

The "1988 World's Most Memorable
Poster" will be displayed in the Center for
Design at the Western Merchandise
Mart. The exhibition, which will premiere
on Tuesday, January 24th, with an open-
ing cocktail reception at 5:30 p.m., is a
collection of winning entries in the 1988
Third Annual International Poster Design
Competition representing the work of
800 artists from 40 countries.
   Nine posters represent the work of
American Designers. Four were produced
by Bay Area Designers Michael Vanderbyl,
Craig Frazier, Tim Brosnan and Michael
Schwab, and Stephan Siehr and Jose Ortega.
Other American winners include Seymour
Chwast, Steff Geissbuhler, James McMullan
and Jim Russek.
   The poster competitions are organized
in association with UNESCO, the United
Nations Educational, Scientific and
Cultural Organization, and are judged on
the basis of creativity, quality of graphic
design, impact, authenticity and global
appreciation.
   The Western Merchandise Mart is
located at 1355 Market Street in San
Francisco, exhibition hours are Monday
through Friday from 10:00 a.m. to
6:00 p.m., for more information call
415/552-2311.

SAARLÄNDISCHES STAATSTHEATER

THEATER
DER LETZTE PLATZ FÜR PHANTASIE

keine
INTENDANTENHERRLICHKEIT
keine
KULTURBÜROKRATEN
kein
VERWALTUNGSWASSERKOPF
sondern
THEATER

MAI 1989

MY HUNDRED CHILDREN

Jude

MONDAY, NOVEMBER 23RD 1987, 9-11PM ET
ON THE NBC TELEVISION NETWORK

HOME FIRES BURNING

THE 160TH PRESENTATION OF THE HALLMARK HALL OF FAME.
STARRING BARNARD HUGHES, SADA THOMPSON,
ROBERT PROSKY, AND NEIL PATRICK HARRIS.
SUNDAY, JANUARY 29, 1989 ON CBS-TV.

戏剧艺术

Alfred Jarry
Ab 9. Febr. '89, Do–So um 20.30 Uhr   **Regie: Wolfgang Anraths**

Ubu
ROi
theater k.
Kurfürstenstr. 8, München, Vorbestellung ab 17 Uhr: Tel. 33 39 33 ● ● ● ● ●

运动中的艺术广告

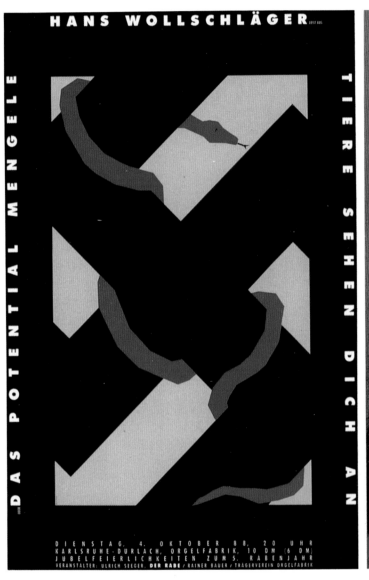

汉斯

歌剧《卡门》广告

宣传广告

日本三菱汽车公司广告

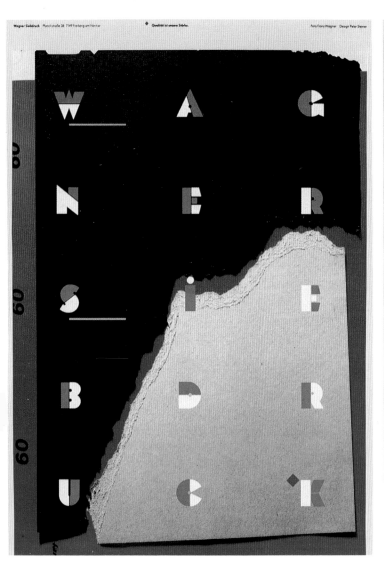

Wagner Siebdruck Planckstraße 38 7149 Freiberg am Neckar

● **Unsere Stärke ist die Qualität.**

Foto Franz Wagner Design Peter Steiner

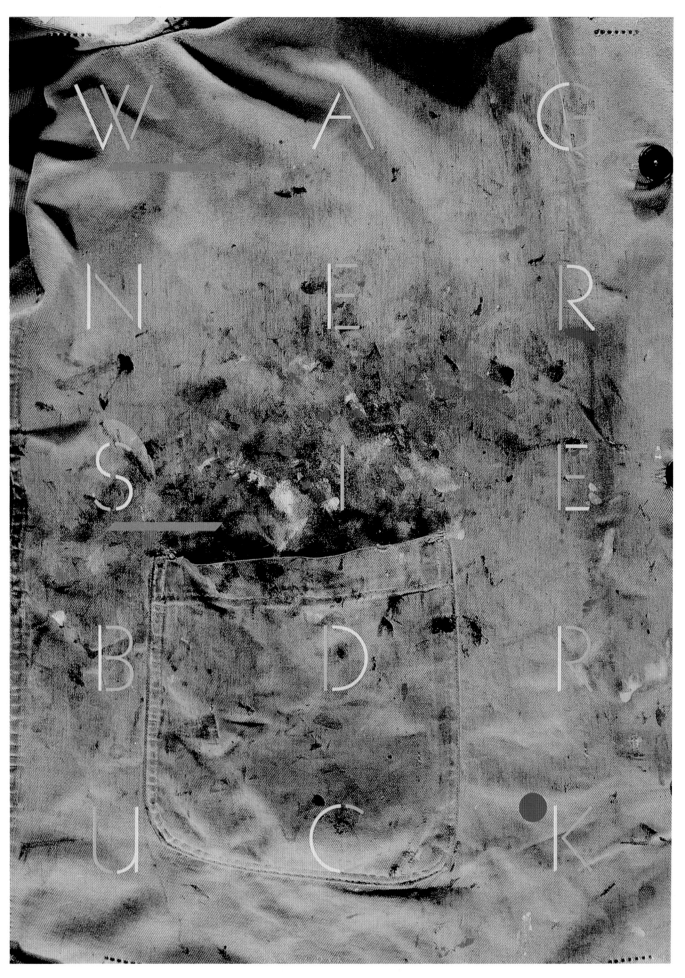

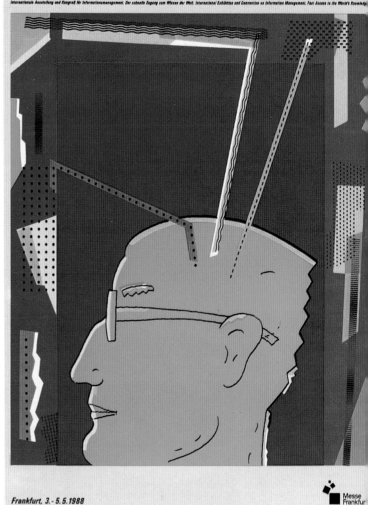

1989 年美国冬季山坡滑雪广告　1988 年法兰克福信息博览会广告

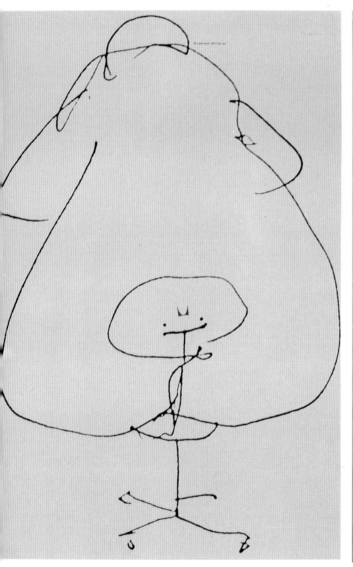

广告 现代工业产品设计展示

意大利风味香肠广告

 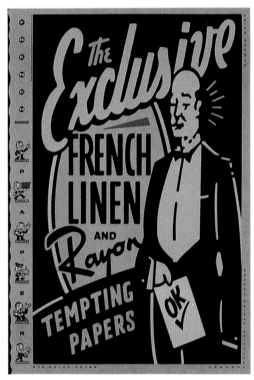 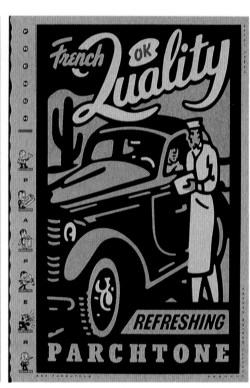

法国产品广告系列

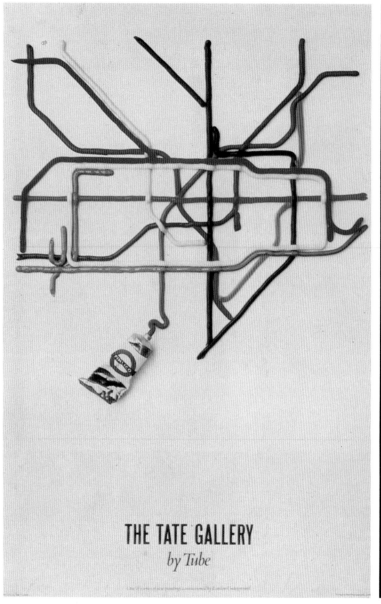

画展广告

宣传广告

AIGA cover show

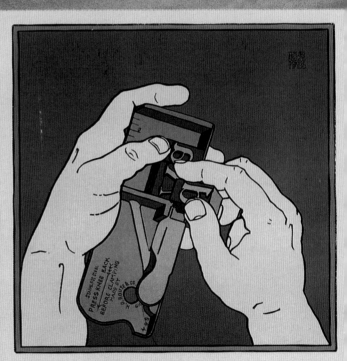

1988:
INTERNATIONAL
YEAR OF
GRAPHIC DESIGN
25TH ANNIVERSARY
ICOGRADA

INTERNATIONAL COUNCIL OF
GRAPHIC DESIGN ASSOCIATIONS·
CONSEIL INTERNATIONAL
DES ASSOCIATION DES
DESIGN GRAPHIQUE

July 3-21, 1989

SWITZERLAND

14th Kent Summer in Switzerland Graphic Design Workshop.

A.D.A.C.
ART·DIRECTORS
& ARTISTS·CLUB
OF SACRAMENTO
2791·24TH STREET SACRAMENTO CA 95818·916·731-8802

88 年平面设计国际年广告

宣传广告

89 年瑞士平面设计创作展示

克拉门托艺术家俱乐部广告

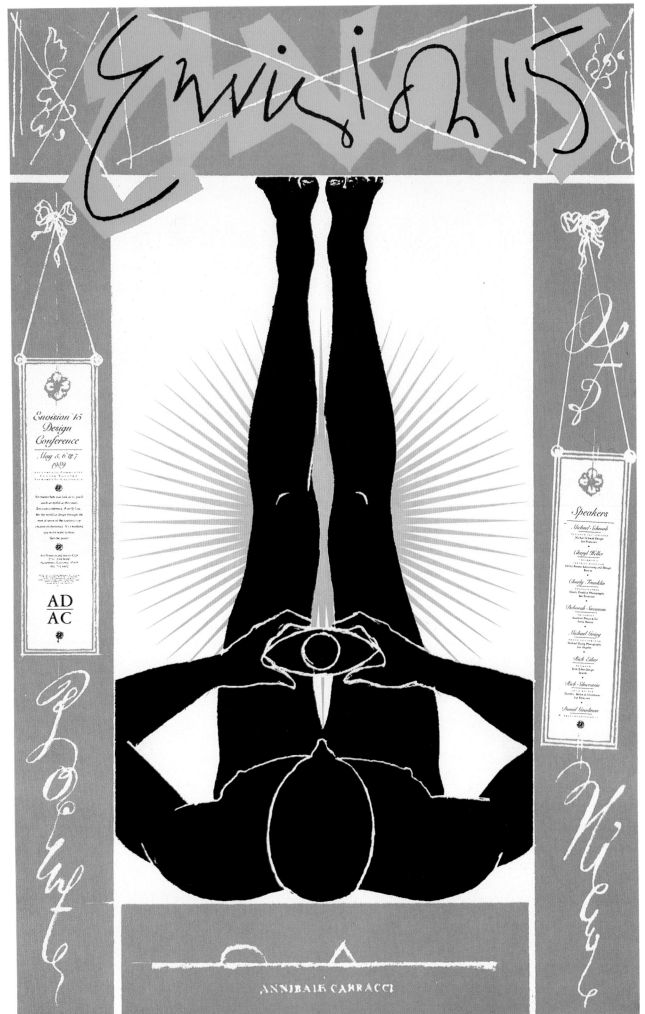

设计会议

宣传广告

宣传广告

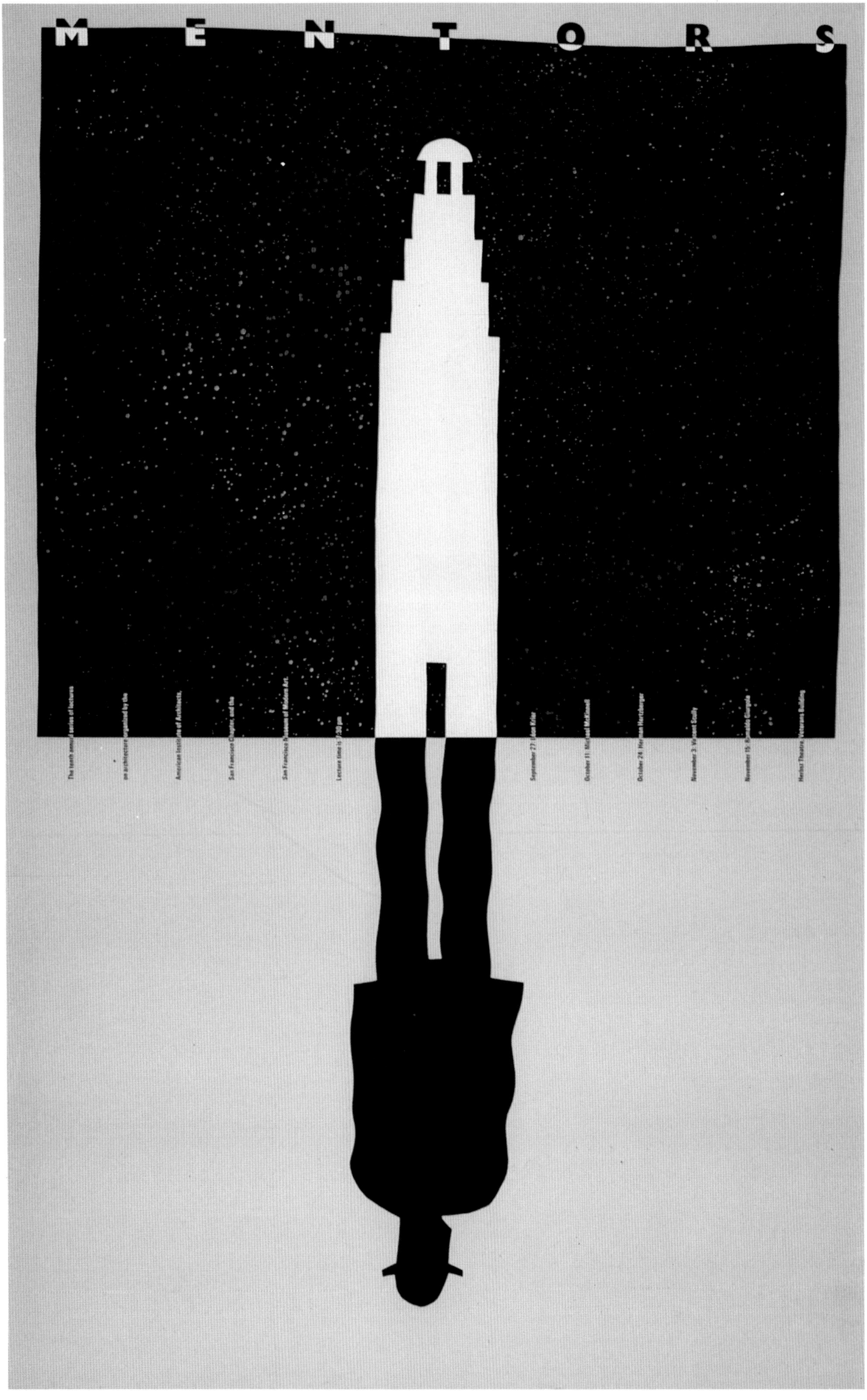

MENTORS

学术讲座广告

The tenth annual series of lectures

on architecture organized by the

American Institute of Architects.

San Francisco Chapter, and the

San Francisco Museum of Modern Art.

Lecture time is 7:30 pm.

September 27: Adam Miller

October 11: Michael McKinneII

October 24: Herman Hertzberger

November 3: Vincent Scully

November 15: Aldo Giurgola

Merino Theatre: Veterans Building

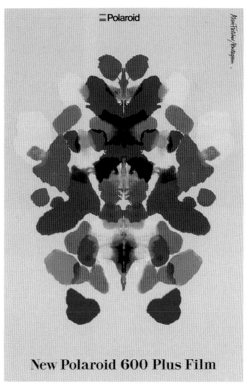

New Polaroid 600 Plus Film

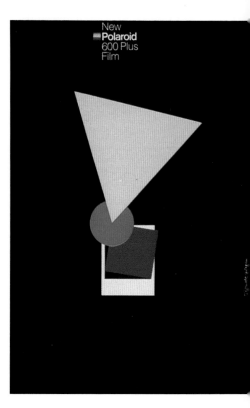

胶卷公司广告

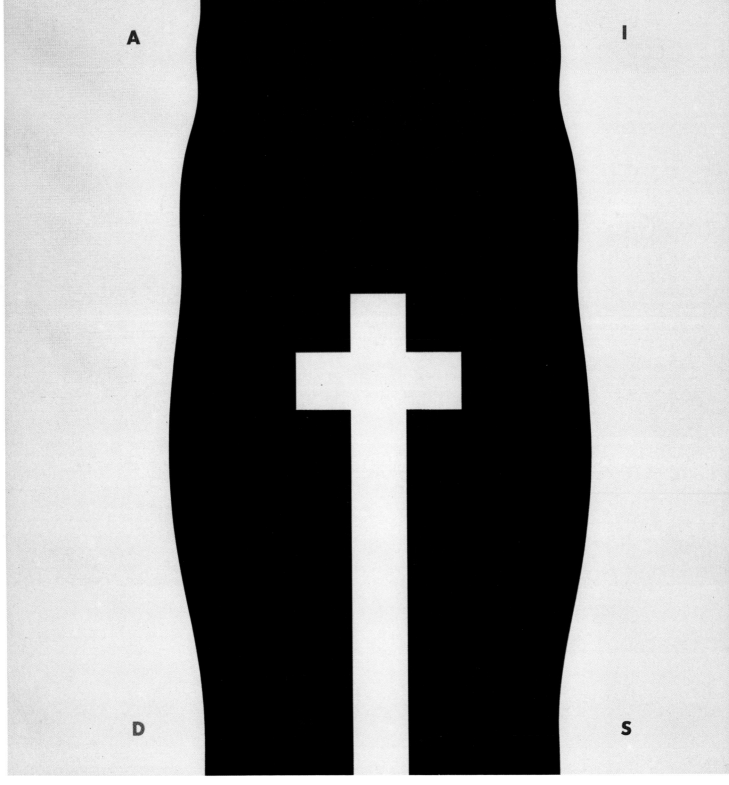

预防爱滋病

C.C.A.C. SUMMER ART — FIND OUT

Enroll in the California
College of Arts and Crafts
(CCAC) Summer Precollege
Program and experience the
excitement and challenge of
one of the nation's best art
and design colleges. With
students from throughout
the country, you will study
with some of CCAC's most
famous art and design
professionals. The intensive
three week program starts
with a week of 2D, 3D,
color and light projects. In
weeks two and three you
may choose an area for
concentrated studio study:
graphic design, industrial
design, painting/drawing,
sculpture, or architecture.
Special activities include
discussion/demonstrations
with visiting artists, drawing
from live models, tours of
art and design studios,
and exploration of the
fascinating San Francisco

Bay Area. CCAC's summer
program is a unique
opportunity to immerse
yourself in the arts, study
variety of media, develop
your portfolio, and find ou
what part the arts will play
in your future. Students a
all levels of artistic ability
are encouraged to apply.
Come find out!
WHO: Students who have
completed grades 10, 11,
WHEN: July 10-28, 1989
WHERE: California College
Arts and Crafts, Oakland
and San Francisco, Califor
(dormitory space available
on the Oakland campus).
For more information, call
write: California College
Arts and Crafts Precollege
Program, 5212 Broadway
Oakland, CA , 94618
In California:
(415) 653-8822
Outside California:
1-800-447-1-ART

ABOUT THE ARTIST IN YO

夏季艺术学校广告

Too much fun isn't always a pretty picture. Party safe.

娱乐

音乐

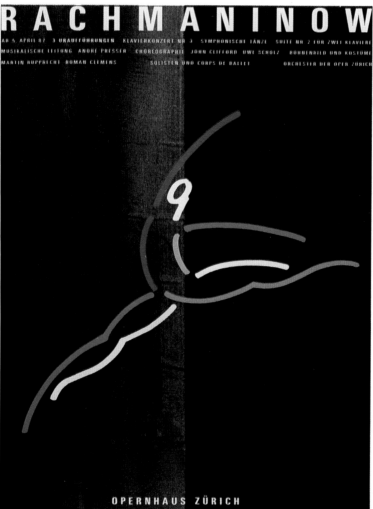

宣传广告

宣传广告

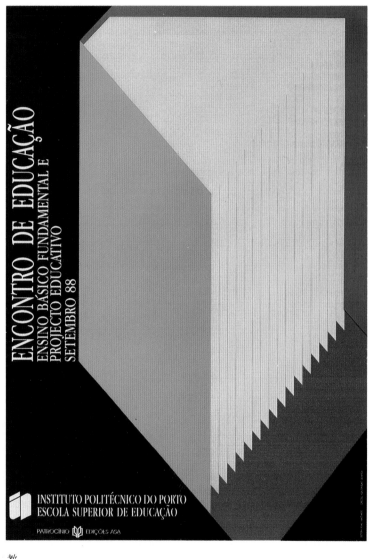

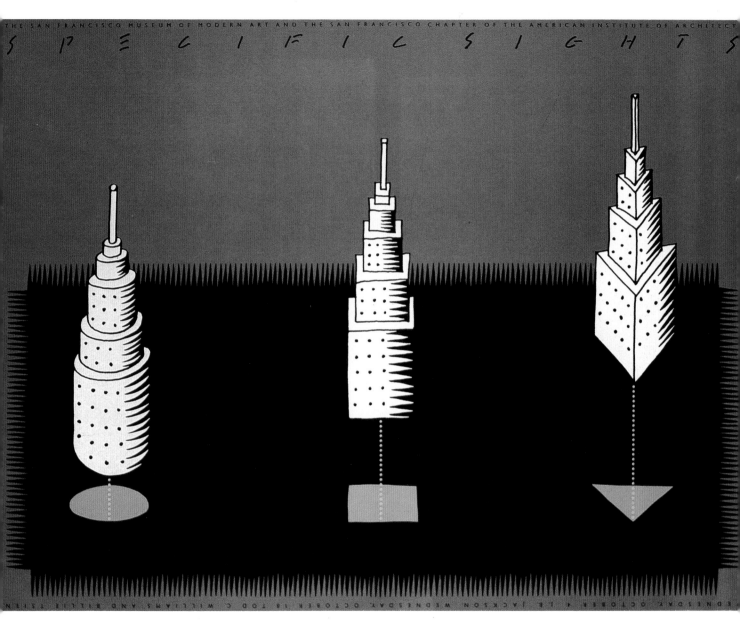

特殊视线——圣·弗兰西斯科现代艺术博物馆广告

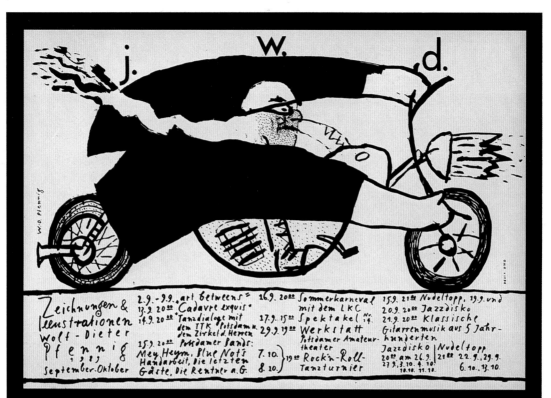

宣传广告

FEBRUARY 23–APRIL 8
19 90
CONTEMPORARY
CZECHOSLOVAK
POSTERS
CITY GALLERY OF CONTEMPORARY ART
RALEIGH, NORTH CAROLINA
SPONSORED BY THE RALEIGH CHAPTER OF THE AMERICAN INSTITUTE OF GRAPHIC ARTS

当代捷克斯洛伐克广告展

阿尔敏霍夫曼平面设计展广告

Armin Hofmann
Graphic Design
Die Neue Sammlung
Di–So 10–17 Uhr
27. 10. 89–
14. 1. 90

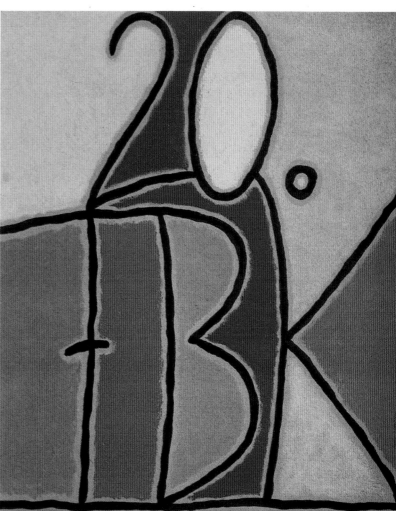

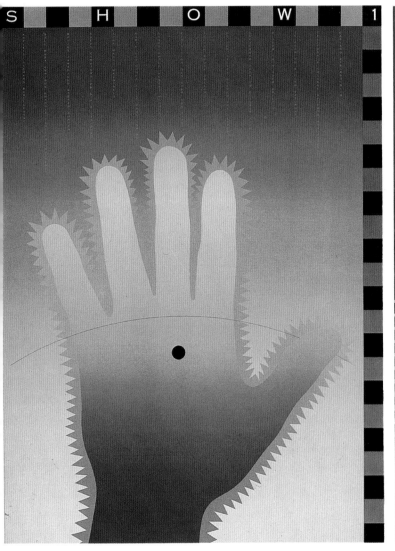

1990 年工业产品设计选

宣传广告

电话

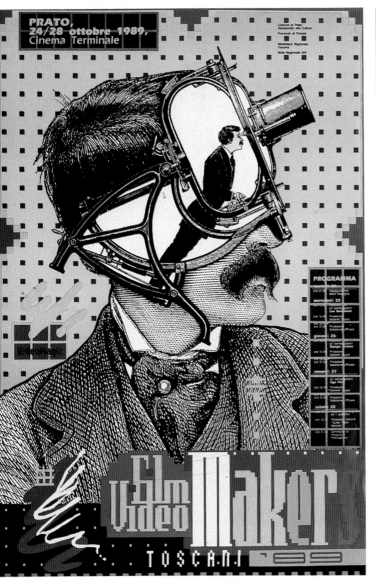

影像市场

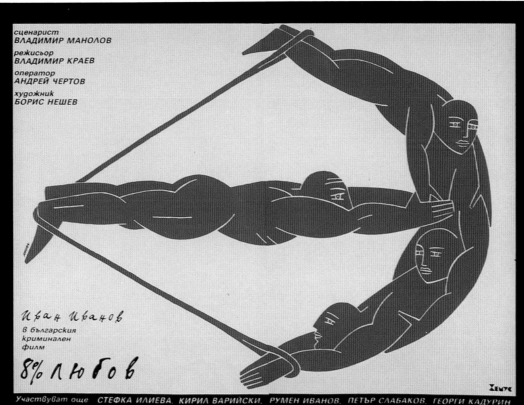

сценарист
ВЛАДИМИР МАНОЛОВ
режисьор
ВЛАДИМИР КРАЕВ
оператор
АНДРЕЙ ЧЕРТОВ
художник
БОРИС НЕШЕВ

Иван Иванов
в българския
криминален
филм

8% ЛЮбоБ

Участвуват още СТЕФКА ИЛИЕВА, КИРИЛ ВАРИЙСКИ, РУМЕН ИВАНОВ, ПЕТЪР СЛАБАКОВ, ГЕОРГИ КАДУРИН

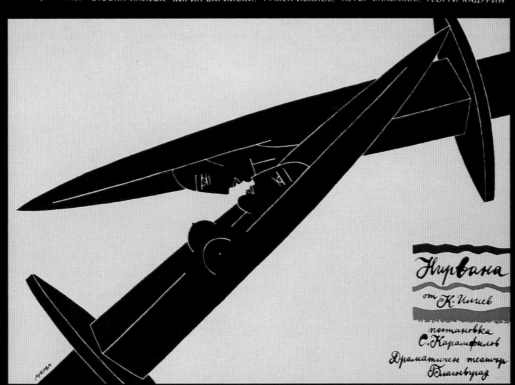

Нирвана
от К. Илиев

постановка
С. Карамфилов
Драматичен театър
Благоевград

广告设计广告

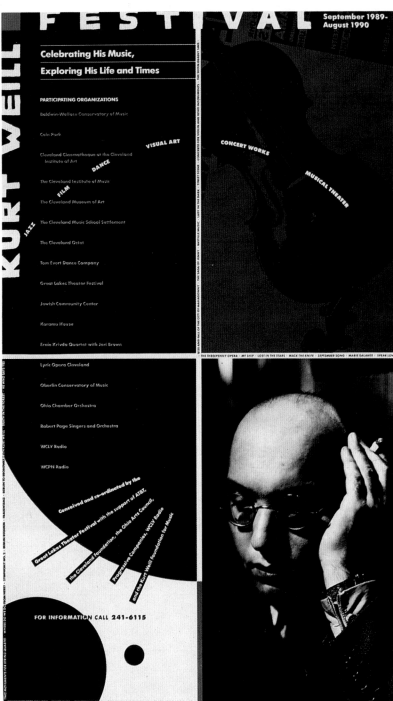

中心剧院戏剧广告　　　　　　　　　　　　KURT WEILL 音乐节

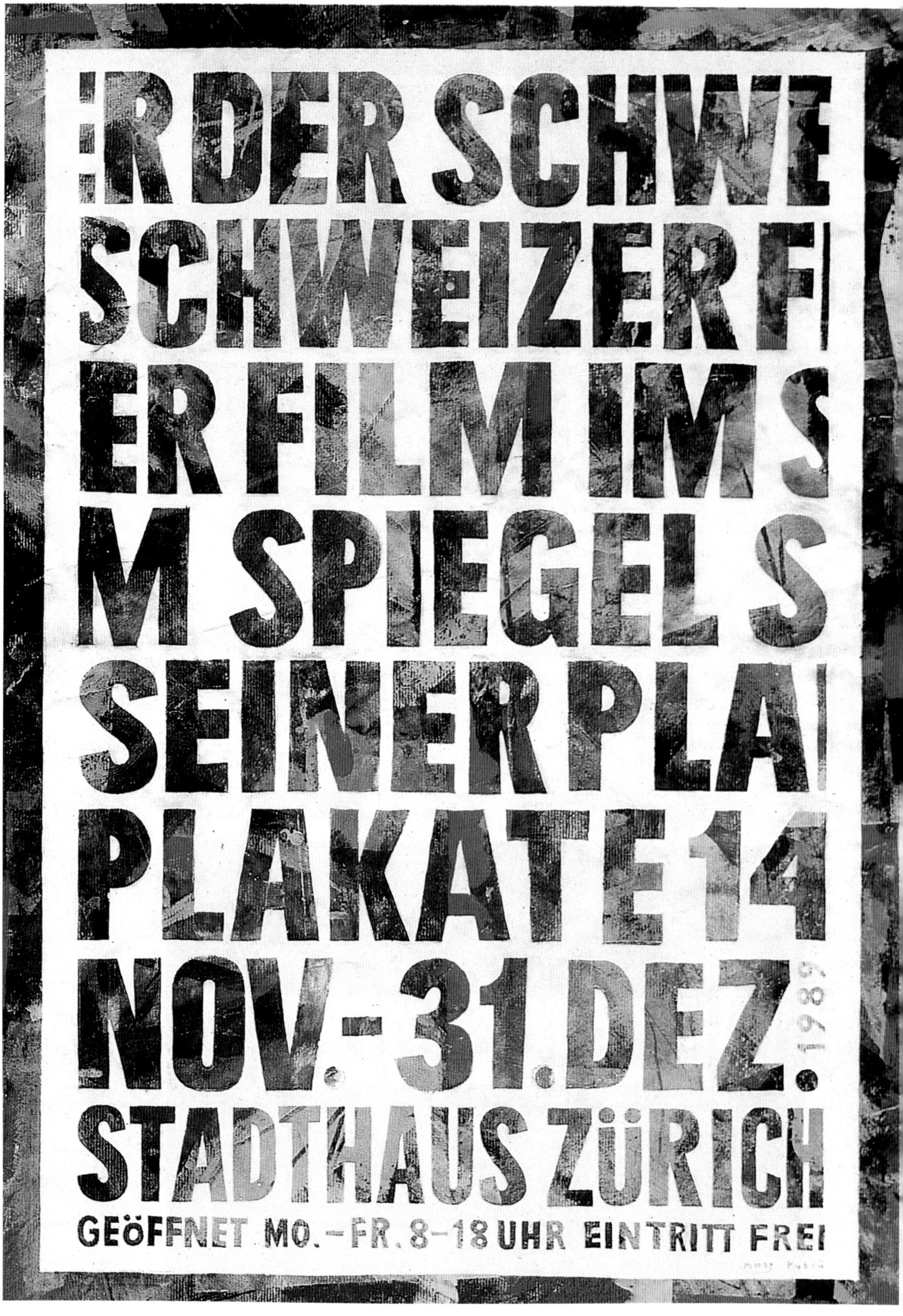
R DER SCHWE
SCHWEIZER F
ER FILM IM S
M SPIEGEL S
SEINER PLA
PLAKATE 14
NOV.-31.DEZ.
1989
STADTHAUS ZÜRICH
GEÖFFNET MO.-FR. 8-18 UHR EINTRITT FREI

新音响、新视觉

萨克斯四重奏

音乐会招贴

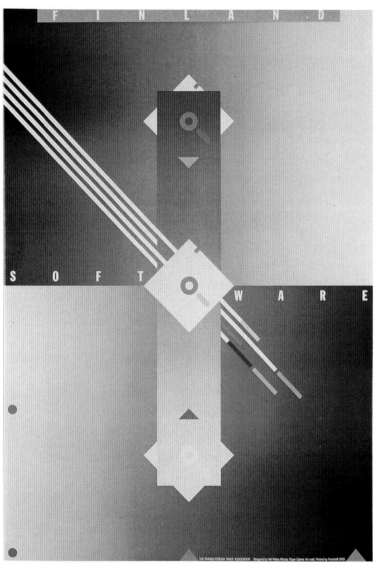

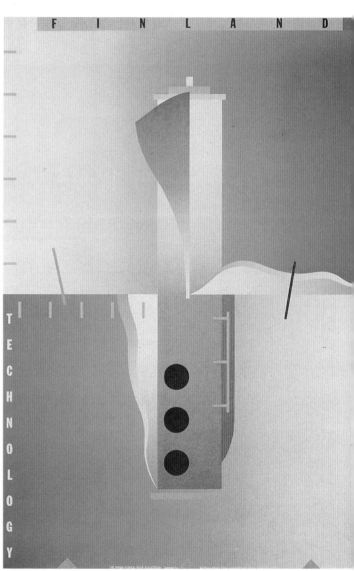

芬兰软件广告

芬兰水下技术广告

宣传广告

Schauspiel

Murray/Boretz
Theater im Hotel
Ballhof
Ab 23. Februar '90

戏
剧

宣传广告

十月

设 计

"月亮公园" 广告

THE ACCURACY TO HIT A BALL ANYWHERE YOUR CONSCIENCE PERMITS.

THE DUNLOP MAX IMPACT RACQUETS.
DUNLOP TENNIS

网球

Racquets for
the aggressive player.
The new Penn wide-bodies,
the latest in a killer line of
mid and oversized racquets,
gloves, bags and balls.

攻击球拍

创新

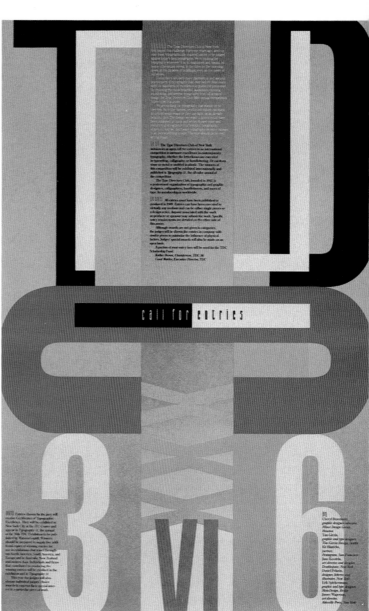

广告

设
计
年
展

突破

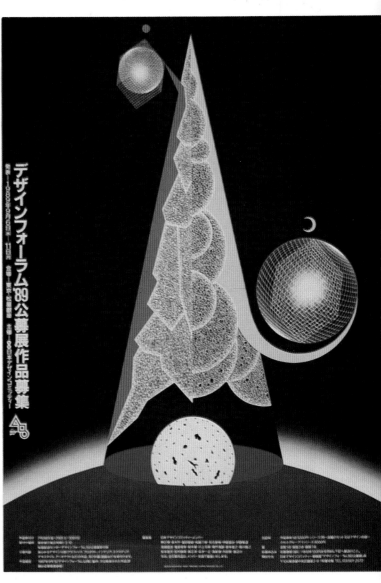

建筑艺术设计　设计讨论会 1989 年公募展作品募集广告

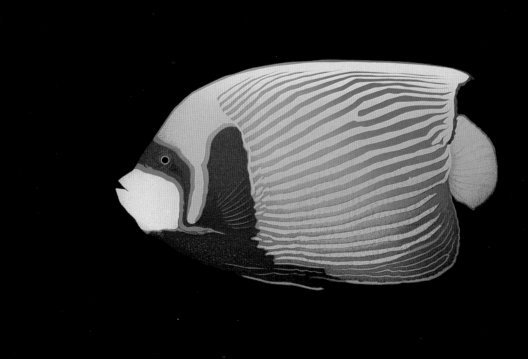

"然"主题设计广告

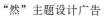

"然"主题设计广告 　　　　　　　舞

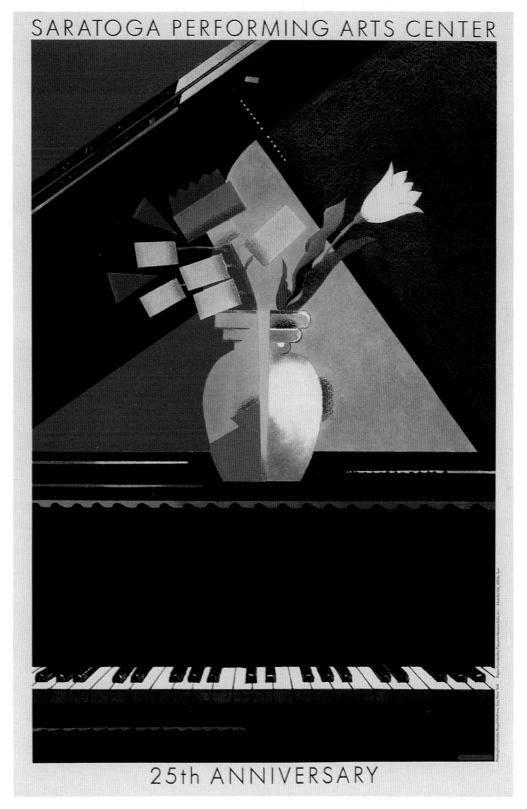

萨拉托加表演艺术中心 25 周年纪念广告

hubert
PATTIEU

ART GRAPHIQUE
edition

艺术图画

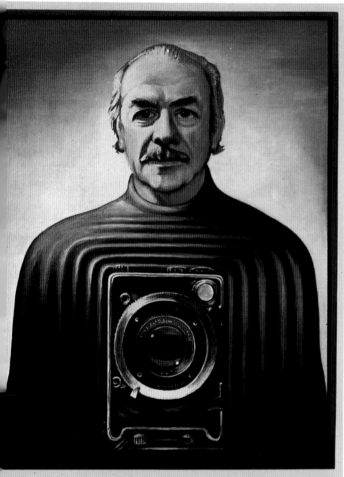

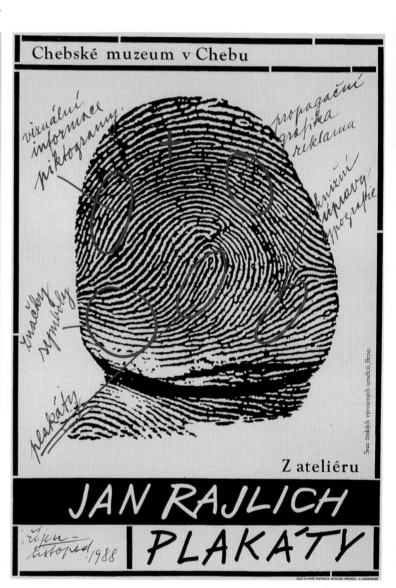

圣诞舞会广告

ouklazhet o deus Chico Mendès.

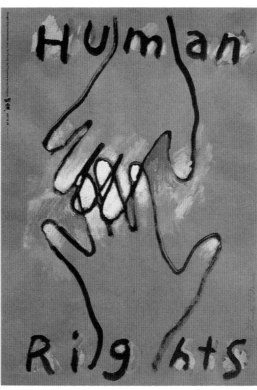

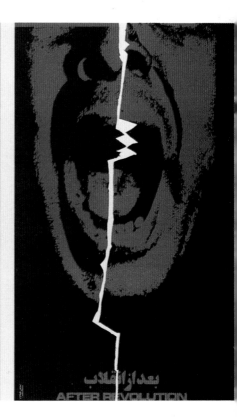

بعد از انقلاب

AFTER REVOLUTION

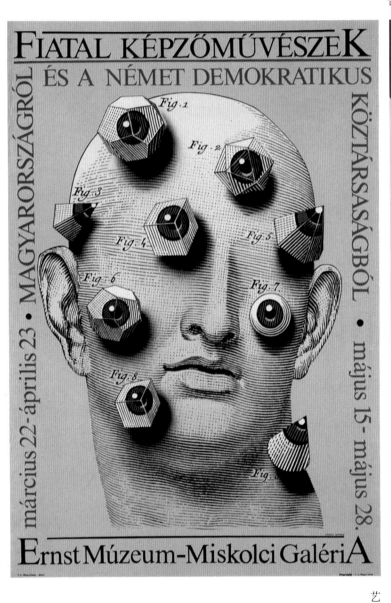

The New York Art Directors Club Per Arnoldi Posters

The 1988 Polaroid Poster Collection 13 to 28 Feb 1989

Alan Fletcher
Pentagram, UK

Bruno Oldani
Norway

David Hillman
Pentagram, UK

Fernando Medina
Spain

Gabor Palotai
Sweden

Grapus
France

Jean-Michel Folon
Belgium

John McConnell
Pentagram, UK

John Rushworth
Pentagram, UK

Mervyn Kurlansky
Pentagram, UK

Michael Vanderbyl
USA

Per Arnoldi
Denmark

Pierluigi Cerri
Italy

Pierre Mendell
West Germany

Richard Donhauser
Austria

Studio Dumbar
The Netherlands

Takenobu Igarashi
Japan

Werner Jecker
Switzerland

Per Arnoldi
Posters

纽约 1988 年偏振片广告陈列广告

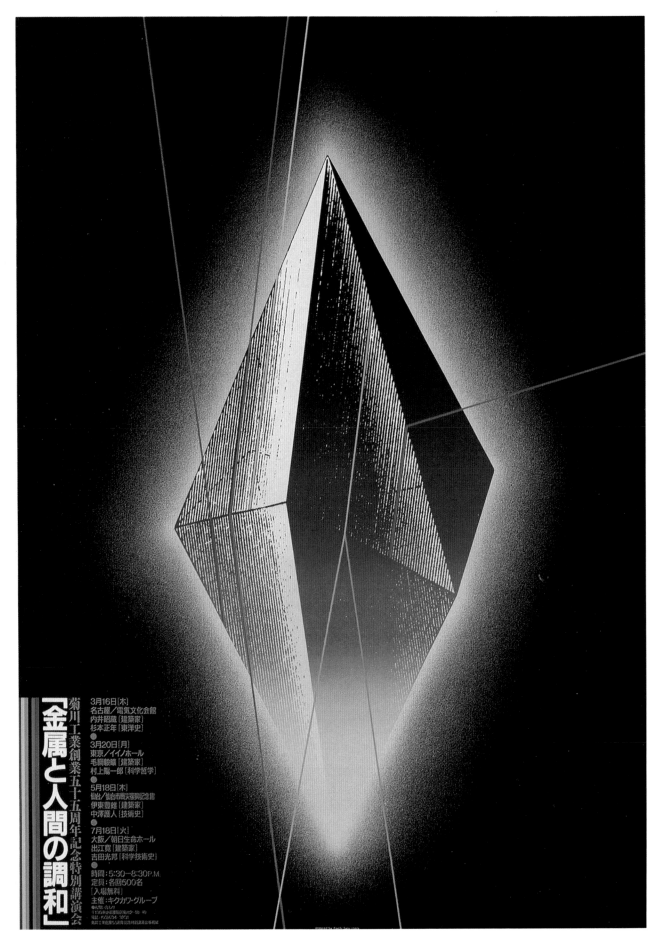

"金属和人类的调和"讲演会广告

宣传广告

苏黎世博物馆广告

'89 设计年广告

宣传广告

女人

THE ART OF COOKING

烹饪

广告

SIMPSON COATED

SHASTA   TAHOE   SEQUOIA   MOJAVE   MESA   CIS LABEL

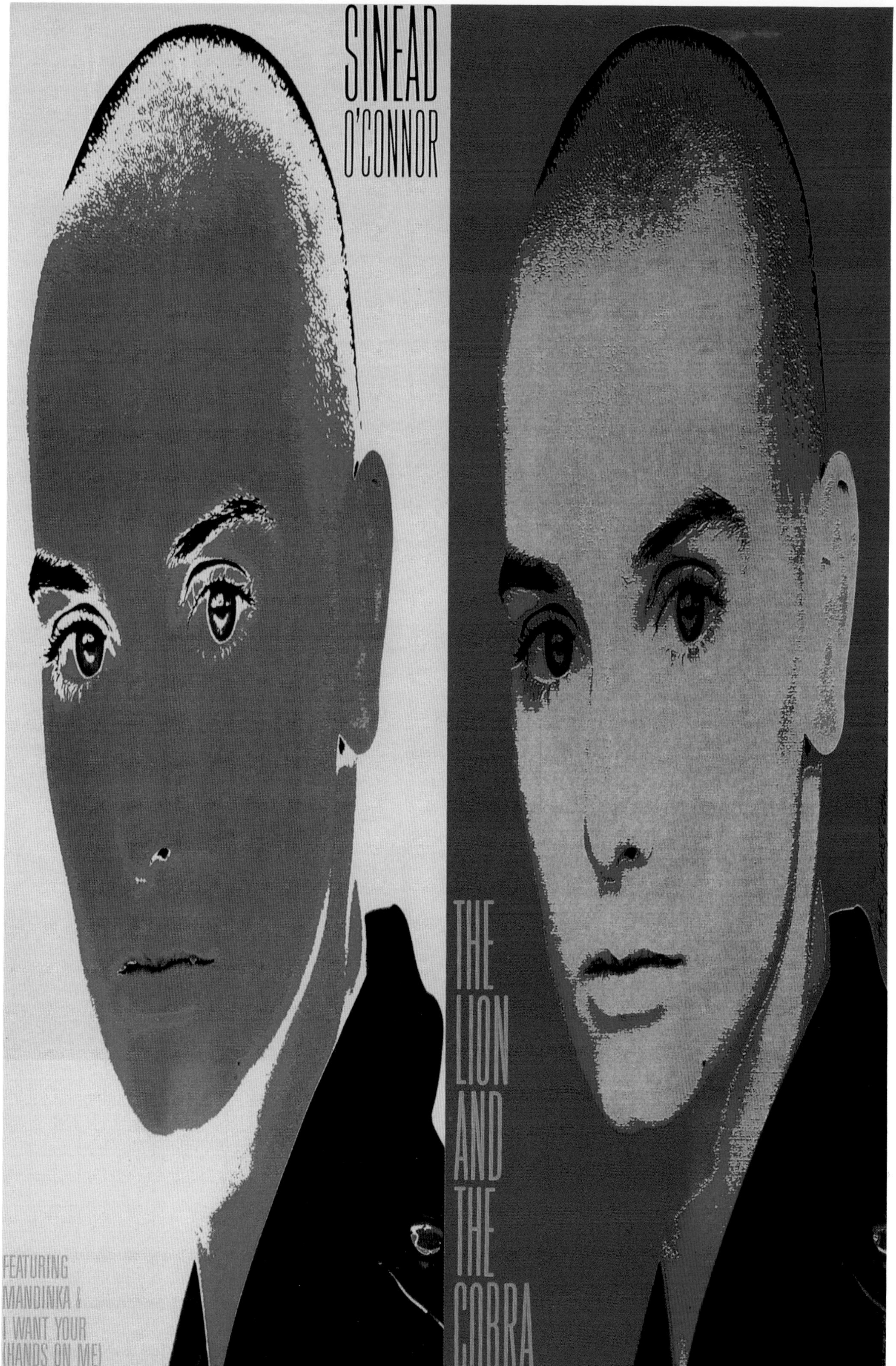

SINEAD O'CONNOR

THE LION AND THE COBRA

FEATURING
MANDINKA /
I WANT YOUR
(HANDS ON ME)

狮子和眼镜蛇

Call for
Entries

The New York Chapter
of the American
Institute of Graphic Arts
invites all members
to submit one 35mm slide
of work of any kind
done in the past year
that represents

Your Best
Shot

The slides will be shown
at the chapter's fourth annual
opening celebration at
The Cooper-Hewitt Museum
Fifth Avenue at 91st Street
on Wednesday, September 16
from 6:30 to 8:30 pm
with food, drink and music

Entry Deadline August 31
See you there!

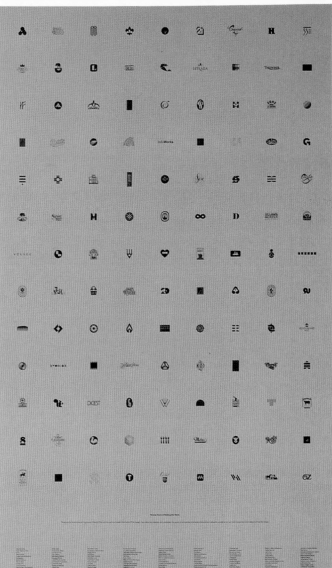

摄影 标志

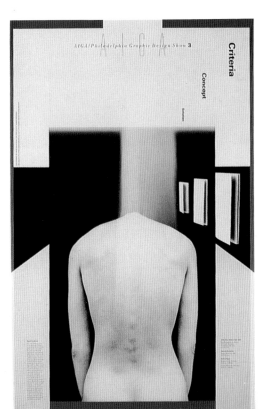

第三届费城平面设计展广告

WOODY PIRTLE
PERFORMING LIVE
THE RINGLING SCHOOL
OF ART AND DESIGN
APRIL 6, 1990

艺术设计学校广告

波士顿设计周

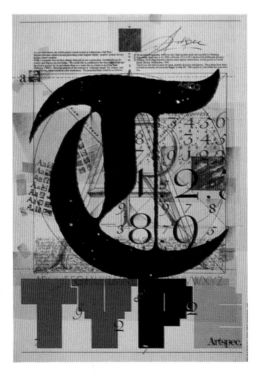

广告

广告

色彩之梦想

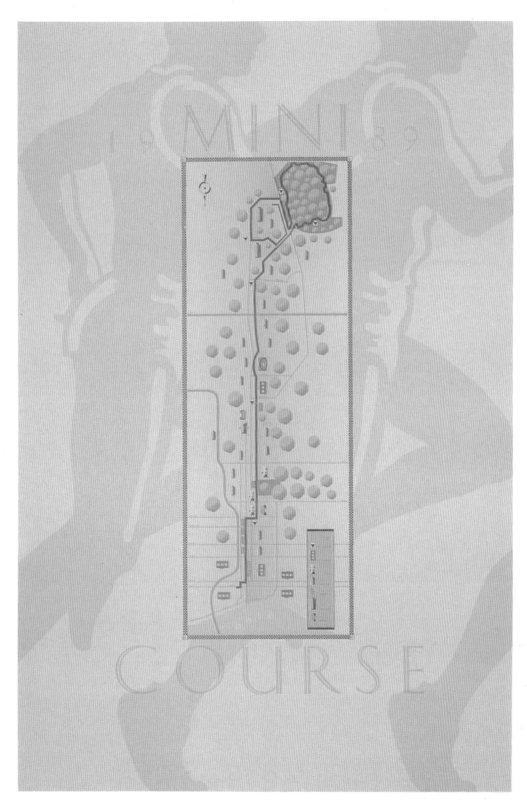

小型之路

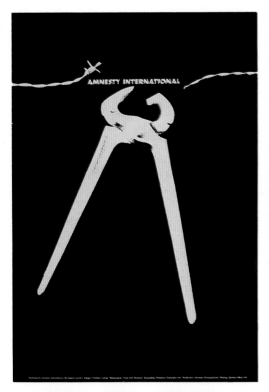

国际大赦

第十四届神奈川艺术节开幕式公演广告　　　　　神奈川艺术节十五周年纪念演奏会广告

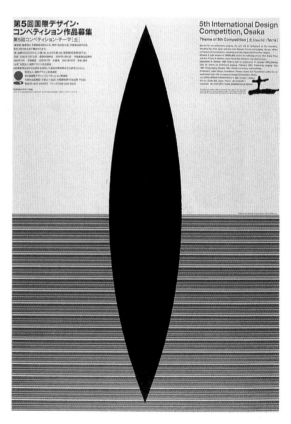

神奈川国际艺术节广告　　　　　　　　　　　日本·第五届国际设计比赛作品募集广告

はな、はな、大好き。

小原流 創流90周年

"花呀、花，我爱你"小原流（插花协会）创流 90 周年广告

日本古典歌舞剧公演海报

当代印刷展

加州艺术

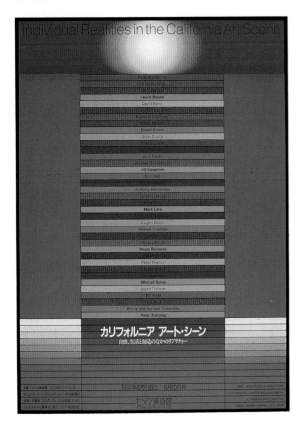

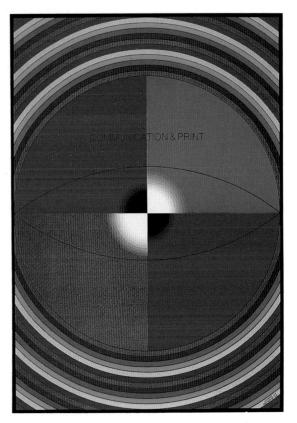

交流与印刷

筑丰的画家群体展广告

LEXIS NO.1 JUN 1989

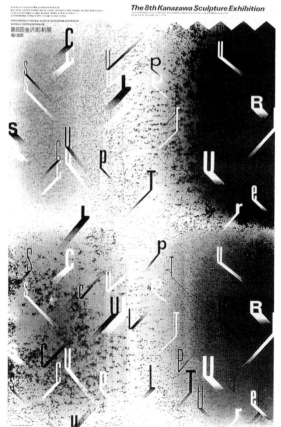

The 8th Kanazawa Sculpture Exhibition

第8回金沢彫刻展
場と空間

雕塑展

野生の植物がどんどん破壊されています。水も土も空気も人類の未来も、あぶない緑の上に乗っているのです。ぜひ治療が必要です。**宇宙船地球号を救え**

緑は、声です。

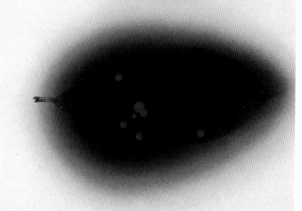

WWF
WWF（世界野生生物基金）は赤十字や
ガン財団と並ぶ世界三大市民運動のひとつです。
人々の良心と寄付によって
人類が生きのびられる自然を守るために
さまざまな活動を進めています。

●設立—1961年　本部—グラン（スイス）　総裁—エジンバラ公フィリップ殿下　●お問い合わせ—WWF Japan Tel.(03)434-2221(代)　●主催—環境庁　外務省　(社)日本青年会議所

绿色的心声

和平

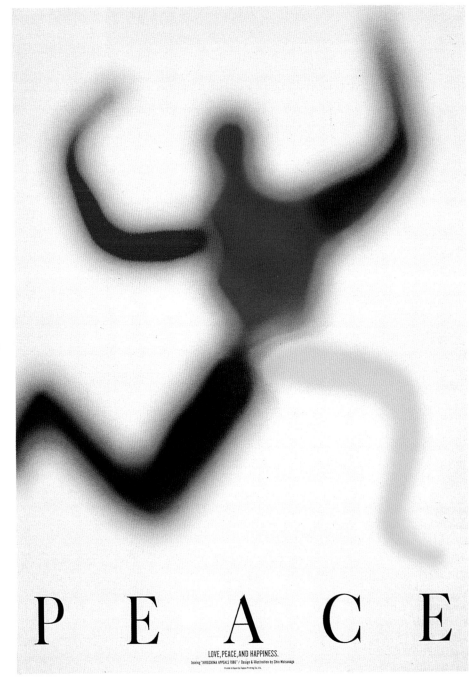

PEACE

LOVE, PEACE, AND HAPPINESS.
Joining "HIROSHIMA APPEALS 1986" / Design & Illustration by Shin Matsunaga
Printed in Japan by Toppan Printing Co., Ltd.

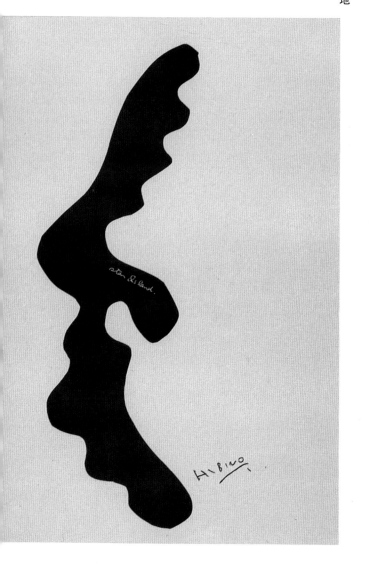

今日も、驚くほど生きる。

Benesse

Benesseは、福武書店の新しいフィロソフィ・ブランドです。　福武書店

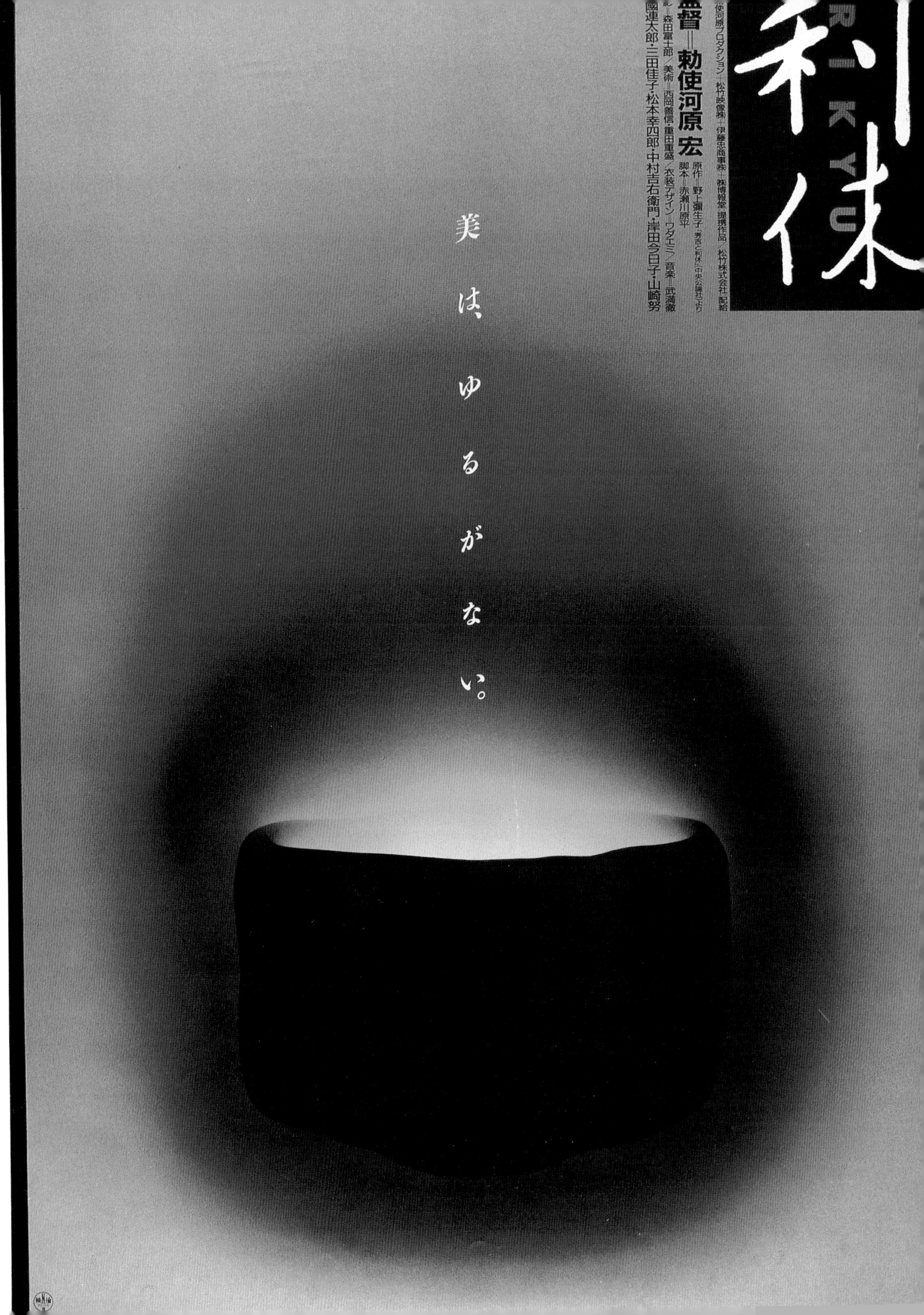
利休
RIKYU
使河原プロダクション＋松竹映像㈱＋伊藤忠商事㈱＋㈱博報堂 提携作品／松竹株式会社 配給
督＝勅使河原 宏
原作＝野上彌生子「秀吉と利休」（中央公論社）より
脚本＝赤瀬川原平
影＝森田富士郎／美術＝西岡善信・重田重盛／衣装デザイン＝ワダエミ／音楽＝武満徹
國連太郎・三田佳子・松本幸四郎・中村吉右衛門・岸田今日子・山崎努
美は、ゆるがない。

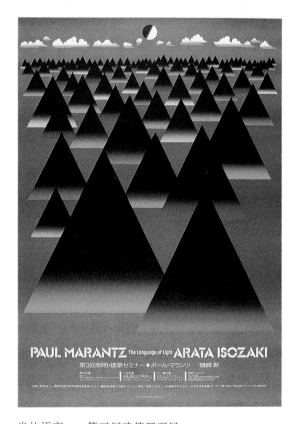

传统与新技术

光的语言——第三届建筑照明展

1984、山本洋司、タイポグラフィック・アート展
人間は文字を未来に残せるのか?
Typographic Art Exhibition 1984 by Yoji Yamamoto   Can mankind pass on letters to the future

竹=Bamboo Pulp

NO MORE WAR
BUT MORE PEACE

Ours is a shrinking world; so the smallest peaceful mind of ours individually will greatly contribute to the whole world peace.

1984年・山本洋司・印刷艺术展

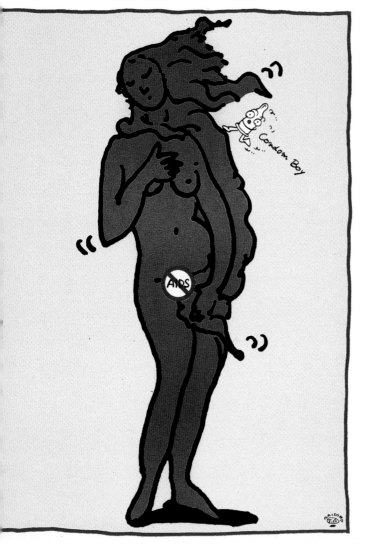

保护野生动物

预防爱滋病

TACTICS
DESIGN

TACTICS
DESIGN

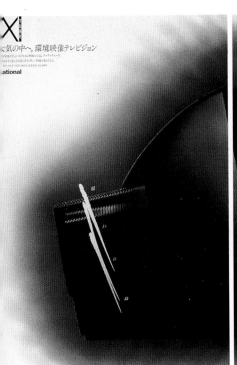

松下电器公司商品广告

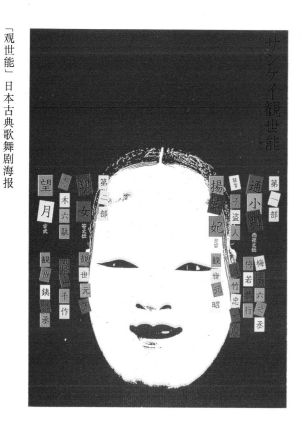

「观世能」日本古典歌舞剧海报

「薪能」日本古典歌舞剧海报

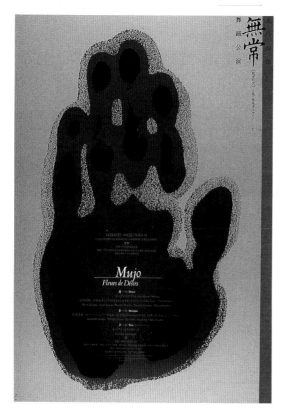

「无常」日本古典歌舞剧海报

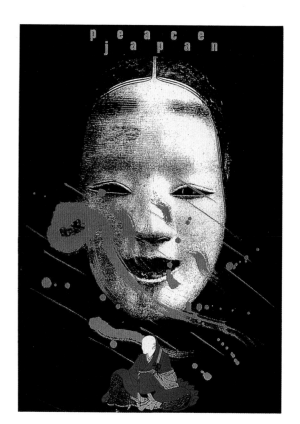

日本和平

口八丁、手八丁、あれはまるで
戦後民主主義のごたる女ごじゃった…

本多劇場提携
みなと座第二回公演

お侠（おきゃん）
生涯を嘘で固めた女

作・演出　岡部耕人

愛本マリ
座美代子
浦勉
川てんし
西和久
子研二

下北沢　本多劇場
'91年4月4日（木）〜18日（木）

みなと座

鼓

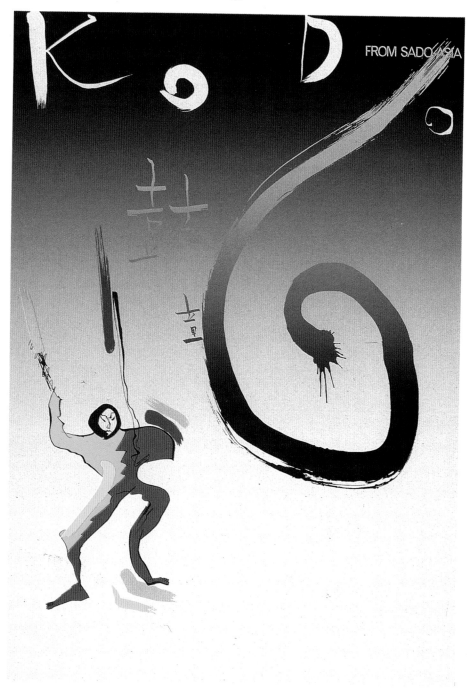

黒船的故事

"保护野生动物"永井一正广告画系列

永井一正广告画展

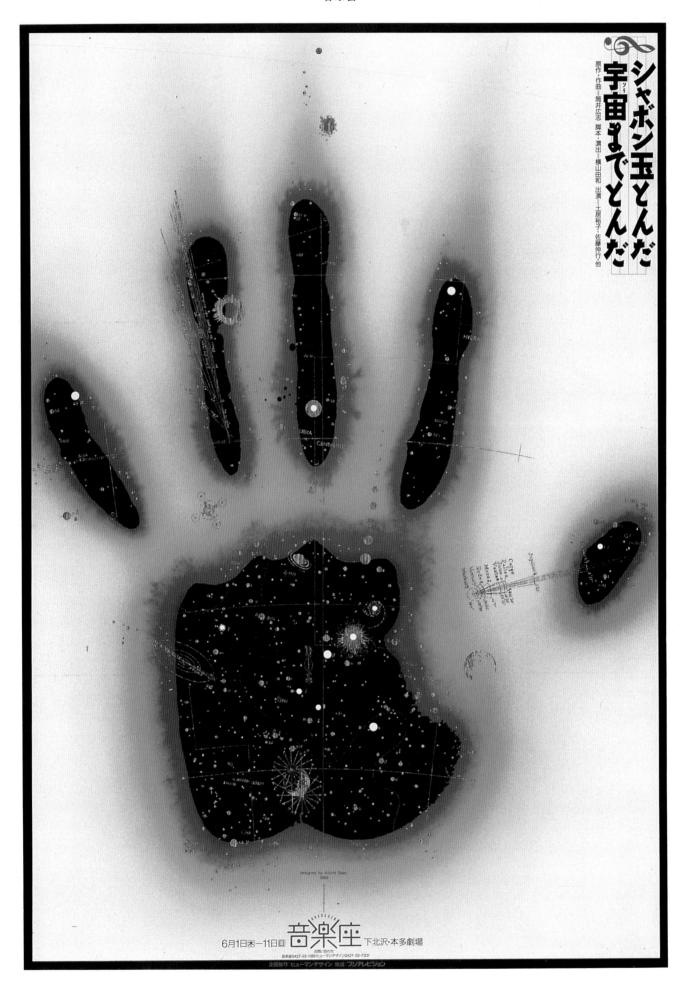

宣传广告

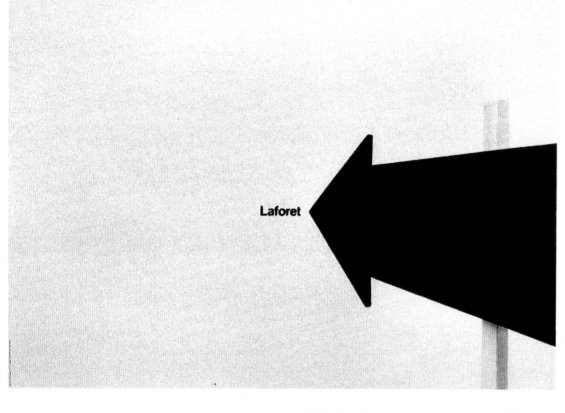

广告

字体设计广告

IBM 电脑公司广告

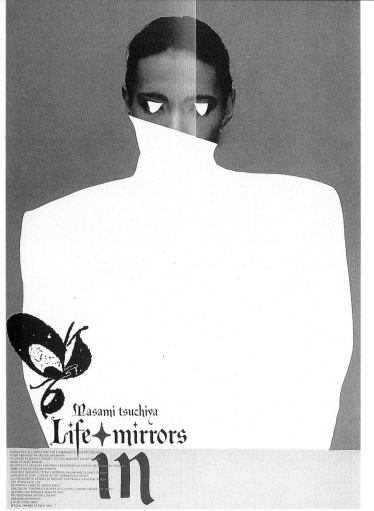

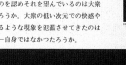

Masami tsuchiya
Life mirrors

第3回コンペティション・テーマ[水]　Theme of the 3rd competition [水; Water]　Thème de ce 3ème concours [水; l'Eau]

2＝現状と疑問　もちろん良貨は悪貨を駆逐すべき
なのだ。しかし現実にはよいものが大衆の無関心や
無理解のために挫折する、といわれてきた。このギ
ャップは、何なのか。大衆に対して憶測するだけで
なく、その根本をえぐるするどいメスを、果してわ

れわれ自身が手にしたかどうか。もしかすると、ほ
んとうによいものを認めそれを望んでいるのは大衆
の側ではないだろうか。大衆の低い次元での快感や
満足感に迎合するような現象を氾濫させてきたのは
むしろデザイナー自身ではなかつたろうか。

迷路はいつも無数にある

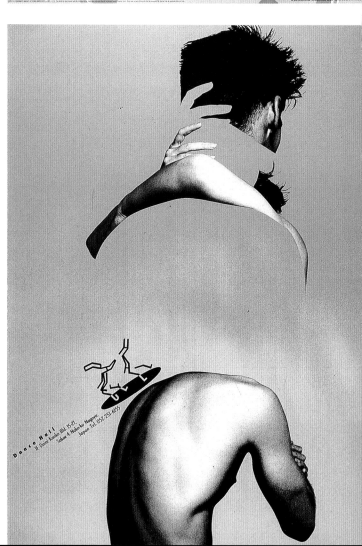

第 10 回东邦学园短期大学・商业设计学科毕业制作展

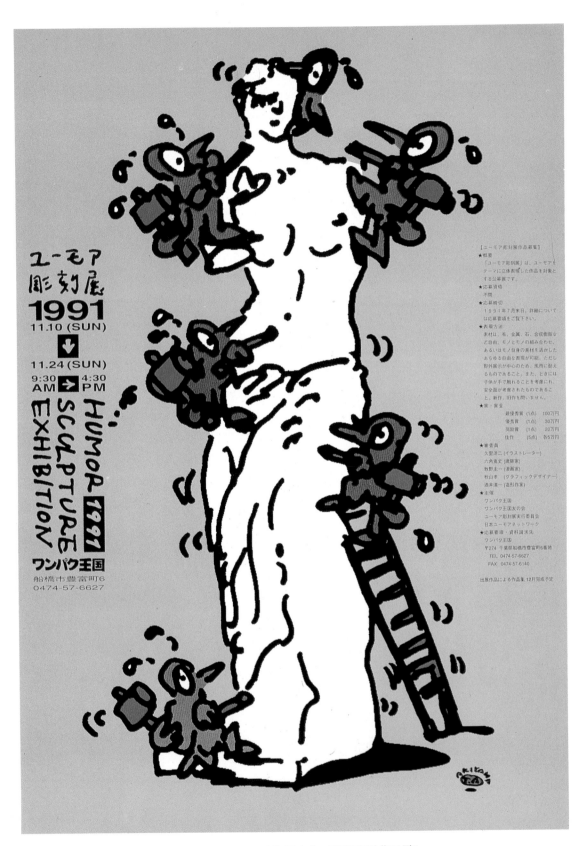

1991年·滑稽雕塑展广告（募集和展览二用）

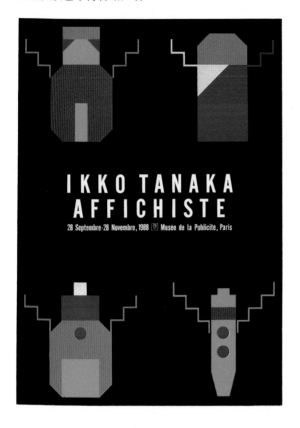

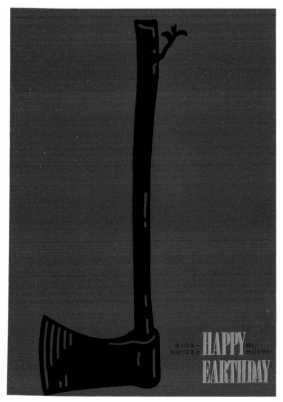

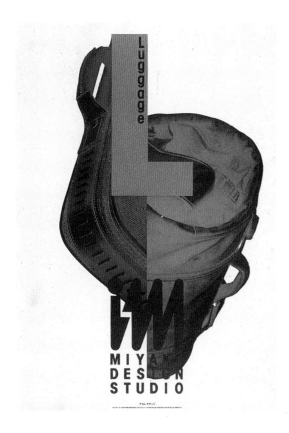

宣传广告